TOY FOOD

Written by Harris Tobias

Illustrated by Janet King

Toy Food
ISBN: 978-1-943314-32-4
Copyright 2021
Casita Press
Charlottesville, Virginia 22903

For my beautiful grandchildren--
Eula, Esme, Lilah, Sadie, Roman and
Atlas.

*O*nce there was a toy maker who lived in a cottage on the edge of a small town not far from here. Now this toy maker made beautiful toys and sold them in his shop. But business was not very good and so the toy maker was very poor and had a difficult time keeping his family fed. There was never enough food for his six children, the toy maker and his wife.

But the children were not unhappy for, after all, they had the most beautiful toys to play with and they pretended that they were rich little boys and girls with the finest toys money could buy.

One year the winter was especially cold and harsh, and as a result there was no business in the shop and, alas, no money with which to buy food.

"Oh dear. Oh dear" cried the toy maker's wife as she looked in the cupboard. "There is only enough food for one more meal. Whatever will become of us?"

"Don't worry," said the toy maker, "something good will happen."

That evening the children ate the last bit of food then retired to the toy shop to play and forget their hunger and the cold in a world of make believe. The old toy maker too retired to his work shop and worked through the night.

The next morning, the children and their mother were roused from their beds by the most delicious food smells. Coming into the kitchen they found the table spread with piles of food.

"But where did all this come from?" the wife asked.

The toy maker smiled and said "Come and sit down and eat and I will tell you everything."

There was no need to ask twice, indeed the children already had their plates piled high with eggs and meats and vegetables. And there was much feasting and joy.

"Now tell us, where did this wonderful food come from?" The old wife laughed with her mouth full.

"Well," said the toy maker, "last night as I was working in the workshop I got the idea of making toys that look like food so that at least we could pretend that we had something to eat. So with wood and paint I fashioned loaves of bread and bowls of potatoes and pitchers of milk. All of the food you see on the table this morning."

"But this is not wood," said the old woman picking up a crust of bread and popping it in her mouth, "This is real".

"That's true," said the toy maker. "But that's not all that happened.

I must have gotten tired working all night for I dozed off and had the strangest dream.

In my dream a young man appeared at my side. I was startled since I had not heard anyone enter the shop. The stranger said that he represented the 'spirit of the toys' and that he knew of our problems and was prepared to help us.

Some weeks later, when the storm passed and the icy winter began to thaw, a customer entered the toy shop and was surprised to find two large dolls and six small dolls all in the likeness of the old toy maker and his family seated around the table. The table was set with many brightly painted dishes of toy food. All of the dolls had contented smiles on their faces but of the living toy maker and his family no trace could be found.

The Spirit of the Toys had kept his promise, he had turned them all into toys.

THE END

Some Other books by Harris Tobias that you might enjoy:

The Lula Belle
Katya & The Crow
At The Robot Zoo
Five Little Froggies
The Adventures of Rocket Bob
The King's Dream
A Wish Too Far
The Broody Little Hen
The Big Fat Counting Book
The Three Chocolatiers
The Three Swords
The Wisdom of Yaqui the Bear
The Catch of the Day
A Wish Too Far
A Child's Book of Riddles
A Prisoner of Beauty
The Stone Apples
Baker's Dozen
Bug Alphabet
Catch of the Day
Farm Song
Stinky Feet
How The Pelican Got Its Beak

How The Zebra Got Its Stripes
A Child's Book of Riddles
Snails, Scales & Animal Tales
Storyland Jack
The Three Brothers
Trumpet The Homeless Troll
A Chanukah Story
DragonSong
And for older readers:
A Felony of Birds
T he Greer Agency
Alien Fruit
Chronon, Time Travel Stories
Hold The Anchovies
Peaceful Intent
The Stang
Dick Danks, The Collected Stories
Assisted
Square Sally in Circletown
How Birds Got T heir Colors
The Amulet of Power
How The Cat Got Its Whiskers
The Adventures of MoonRivet
The Turtles Ball

All Titles are available on
Amazon in print and as e-books.